I0669637

M. F. Bentley

Bad Day on the Farm

M. F. Bentley

Bad Day on the Farm

ISBN/EAN: 9783337413613

Printed in Europe, USA, Canada, Australia, Japan

Cover: Foto ©Andreas Hilbeck / pixelio.de

More available books at **www.hansebooks.com**

Bad Day on The Farm,

BY

M. F. BENTLEY.

--ILLUSTRATED.--

Herald Print, Potsdam. N. Y.

POEM.

"The milk had almost ceased to flow. The finishing stroke was near. When quicker by far, than a "shooting star" Dan landed on his ear."

PREFACE.

To my fellow Farmers and the Public in general I dedicate this "Little Work," with a hope, though prehaps born of weakness, that it merits a share of public patronage. And as I take this tiny "Craft" from the work shop of my mind, as I loosen the moorings that have held it at "Home," and push it out as it were upon the sea of minds, unfurl its sails to be caught by the breezes of public approbation; I am well aware that the same canvas thus spread may be met with the adverse winds of public criticism. But whether it shall make a successful voyage, be wafted by propitious breezes, or whether it will be swamped among the angry billows of public condemnations, now remains with itself. As with the material ship, it remains to its construction, the Captain and his Crew. The Sailors on board this "Craft" are all "Jolly Country Lads," their duties, their pleasures, their wit, are of the Farmer kind. The Pictures hung in its State Rooms and along its Dining Hall are Home and Country scenes. Its Cabin is furnished and decorated in a rustic manner. On the center table lays "God's Word" untrammeled by any Sect, which I trust is the Chart by which She sails, and thus I "Launch Her" upon the Great Ocean of Human Minds, asking the kind forbearance of an indulgent public

M. F. B.

ARGUMENT.

The scene of this Poem may be supposed to have happened on any New England Farm, in the month of July, and in Haying Time. The time occupied is one day of twenty-four hours, commencing with the setting of the sun in the evening, and ending with the going down of the same the following night.

BAD DAY ON THE FARM.

It was in July and haying time
Just at the close of day,
I had fed the pigs and done the chores
And turned the cows away;
I says to wife, "Tomorrow morn
At precisely four by the clock,
I must make a break and not be late
For I have lots of hay in the cock."

I went to bed and how I dreamed
I dreamed in ryhme and prose, ·
I scarcely got any rest at all
For fear I would over doze;
It was the very longest night;
Would morning never come?
I laid on one side and said, "O, Dear!"
On the other and said, "I Vum!"

The alarm went off and up I sprung
All in the twinkle of an eye;
Put on my pants, my boo's, my hat,
Went out and viewed the sky;
I whistled for my shepherd dog
But at my call he did not come,
So for the cows I scampered off
On a dog trot,—a farmer's run.

I found them all within the lot,
But scattered they were all over,
And bent on feeding to the last
As if they were in clover.
I ran around the whole outside
Like the Cow boys on the plains,
But ere I had started one a rod
She went to feeding again.

O how I hollered! how I yelled!
Until my throat was sore,
I thought of every-thing that's *bad*
(Forgive me if I swore.)
And when I had them in the barn
And all securely tied,
I found that one was missing still
So off for her I hied.

And at the very farthest end
O bless her peaceful soul,
A resting in the fullest content
She lay behind a knoll.
"Get up Old Brin! you lazy scamp!
I know you are somewhat lame,
But you must hustle to the barn
For I see it looks like rain."

Now when them cows they all were milked
And we our breakfast had ate,
I saw by glancing at the clock
That we were two hours late.

I said to Dan, my right hand man,
"Now catch them horses quick,
I saw them when I got the cows,
They are down there by the creek."

" Get up old Brin, you lazy scamp."

Now Dan spoke up and thus he said;
"I know I should have told,
I broke the wagon tongue last night
But was afraid that you would scold.
"I will send right over to the Deacon's
And get his wagon if I can,
He's got two, he will lend us one;
For he is a very clever man."

Back came Dan without the nags,
His face was looking tragic.
"They are not there I do declare
It beats the furies magic."

Cries I, "It does beat Father Time
It beats *all places hot,*
Pox take their jumping hides!
They are in the Deacon's lot."

We finally got them jumping nags,
We borrowed the wagon too,
Our Hay-rack would not fit it,
But then we made it do,
Already we were, and about to start,
When up came neighbor Fry,
And Oh! his anger it was hot,
And his wrath was boiling high.

"*Is that your dog?*" he yelled in tones
That caused my soul to wonder,
"*The Miserable Whelp! the Whining Cur!
Oh Lightning! Blixens! Thunder!*"
"Yes that's my dog my neighbor dear,
Now what have you to say?
At least the tax upon that dog
For years I have had to pay.

"Yes, that's the color, black and white,
Yes, that's the dog as sure as death,
There is no mistake, I have it right,
He soon will die for want of breath."
"Now neighbor Fry ain't you a man?.
Don't vent your spite upon that dog
For if you do, I swear to you,
"You'll lay beside him like a log."

"He has chased my sheep, and tore their wool
The lambs are for their mother crying,
But alas for them, and alas for her,
She is somewhere dead or dying
And I will kill that dog upon the spot,
Or I will some future day,
Unless you settle up this hash
And the damage quickly pay."

"Now if that dog your sheep has chased
I will tell you how to manage,
When you have well made out your case,
Why then I'll pay the damage.
Stop swearing here till the air is blue
With oaths that make me quiver,
Take my advice and hie you home,
Take something for your *liver*.

Drive on the team and let them zip,
We can wait for no more sputtering,"
And as we flew, the wind it blew
The echo of his muttering.
The wind it blew a perfect gale
From the south it came direct,
You could scarcely land a forkfull
Without its being wrecked.

A spiteful gust it took my hat
I thought I would have to yield,
When next I saw that hat of mine
It was clear across the field.

It needed a School House full of boys
To hold that hay in place,
It needed the arm of Hercules
With Sampson's for a brace.

We finally got what we called a load
But what a horrid thing,
It looked like a March Day on a spree
The wildest day in Spring.
Would we ever land it in the barn?
Was no question for a jury,
But whether we had strength enough
To war against this fury.

For it hung all over on one side,
Like a wasp's nest on a tree,
And looked like a Hedgehog just returned
From a Hedgehog bum or spree.
Now Dan I'll carefully drive the team,
You boost from the leeward side,
And we will do our level best
To homeward make it ride.

Slowly we moved and careful too,
I had the best of a team,
In the wind there was a gentle lull
There was hope for us it seemed.
When all at once came a sudden jog,
And then a tremendous slide,
And that hay it lay upon the ground
And I lay by its side.

" And that hay it lay upon the ground, and I lay by its side."

I picked me up, I stared around,
But I saw no stalwart Dan,
Nor was he anywhere to be found
Around all that countraband.
I heard a low and moaning sound,
It came from near my feet,
And when I had my Dan dug out
He was as white as a sheet

Just then my Wife came running out
Came running down the lane,
Cries she: "The cows they have all got out
They are tramping down the grain.
The wind has blown the fence all down
It is flat, as griddle cakes.
There is nothing to hinder their getting out"
Cries I, "Confound their Pates!"

"Dan, to the barn you take the team
And we them cows will chase"
Dan was muttering Nouns and Adjectives
All in the Objective Case.
The Adjectives were *Proper*
If used in a *proper* sense,
But the way that Dan combined them
There are some who'd take offence.

Last Winter I read a Paper
It was of a modern farming tone,
It advised the freer use of brains
To save our muscle and bone.
It told of a new born Oat
As yet, but little known to fame
It told of its egregious weight
And the prodigious yield of the same.

It gave the name of a "Party"
Who resided in a distant State,
That they invited correspondence
And for "orders" they did "wait."

It told the price we would have to pay
By the bushel it was a V,
And though at first it might seem large
That in the end we'd "see."

There would be money in the "project"
It would increase a thousand fold,
That "Nothing ventured, nothing gained"
Was an adage true, if old,
And when the "neighbors" saw them "Oats"
And how stout that they did grow
They would want them all for seed next "Spring"
They would "Buy them in the blow."

The argument was convincing
To me I do confess.
I wrote: "You may send to me a bushel
You may send it by 'Express'
I do not know your Company
Nor neither do you know me,
And for mutual good and surety
You may mark it C. O. D."
Now when that Bill I came to pay
You may bet I was perplexed,
For instead of little over V
It took most all an X.
I took my Chemistry from the shelf
And said, "Good Bye, to aches and pains
Let others use their muscle and bone
But I will use my brains."

"For instead of little over a V, it took most all an X."

I found therein that our Earth was made
Of many a Latin word,
That when the soil was minus one
To try a crop it was absurd.
I found that the soil that I did till
Manipulated, handled, worked,
Was composed of many Chemicals
I always 'sposed 'twas "dirt."

And if the Lord who made our Earth
I ad left some part undone,
Been partial to some certain spot
And slighted some other one,
It became my duty as a man
Of a moderning farming tone,
To supply that part with my own hand
With Guano and Dust of Bone.

I learned that the stuff that adhered to my boots
And which at home I tracked upon the floor,
And which My Wife had said; " *Was mud*"
I found was something more,
That if exposed to heat and rain
And the action of the frost
And the supplying of some "certain part"
That had by chance been lost,—

That I could obtain far better crops
With these helps at command,
Than to take it in its natural state
As it rolled from God's own Hand,
And I made a vow right then and there
And by that vow I swore,
I would give them oats the very best spot
That I could find out door.

I would find a spot where Nature had
Her very finest done,
And then with art I'de fix it up
'Till it was Number One.

I would get manure of Modern Stamp
Those "Patented Eighty-Four,"
I would get Guano from the Isles
And Sea-Weed from the Shore.

I searched my farm from end to end
Made Chemical tests of the same,
And found the very richest spot,
For growing high priced grain.
I measured off just eighty rods
For this my *Baby Plot*,
It was in the very farther end
Of my most farther lot.

And on one pleasant afternoon
Quite early in the season,
I committed them oats to Mother Earth
And then commenced to reason.
I figured up manure and cash,
My labor with muscle and bone,
And then threw into the common sum
My brain work, 'twas my own.

And I thought so then and I have from hence
And I do as I write these lines,
That instead of sowing common grain
I was scattering silver dimes,
But if they only bore their fruit
That lucre for which we strive,
Then I'd be glad, that I'd complied
With what was Advertised.

The clouds descended, the showers came
The sun gave down its light,
And with Nature's elements all combined
Them oats soon hove in sight.
When first I saw them peeping up
It was early in the morn,
I says to Wife when I went up
That my '*Pet Child*' is born.

And day by day this "*Baby*" grew,
In figure I rocked it too and fro,
And when I had nothing else to do
I stood and watched it grow.
I thought so then and I think so now
As I this subject throtle,
If I am permitted the figure of speach,
I brought it up on the "Bottle."

I hung around this sequestered spot
It was my souls enchanter,
I showed it to my many guests
And with them all did banter.
I saw it last on yesters eve
And it was well appearing,
Tall and stout, with color good
Just putting on "Head-Gearing."

That *Child* it died—at 10 to-day
It was *Murder in the First Degree*,
Crushed to death, by the teeth and feet
Of thirty cows on a spree.

Yes, cruelly murdered, cut off from life
In the pride of Youth and Promise,
And when Dan and I arrived on the scene
I was both mad, and astonished.

There stood those thirty murderers

With eye-balls glaring wild,
As if a gloating oe'r the wreck
Of this my own " *Pet Child*."
They passed through clover of inviting sweet
By grain of the common kind,
But never stopped until they reached
This enchanted "spot" of mine.

Yes there upon them "Eighty Rods"
Them thirty murderers stand,
But every spark of life has fled,
There is nothing left, but the land.
Now up and down that lot they fly
Those breakers of the law,
Pursued by men and dog in haste
Oh how they all did claw?

They ran, they cantered, they galloped
With their tails swung in the wind;
They looked like a wild herd on the plain
Pursued with fire behind.
Yes up and down that lot they flew
In a wild chaotic prance,
And the tune to which they all kept step
Was the same the Wild Men dance.

Yes up and down that field they went
They knew where they got in;
They could not see it now you know,
That's just the way with sin.

They flew like "demons" at the stakes
As if they owed them spite.
Took on their horns a wad of hay,
As they ran onward in their flight.

I chased them "murderers" till I tired
My breath was almost gone,
And then from dire exhaustion
Sank down upon a stone.
And when I had well caught my breath
So I could my thoughts direct,
I think they'd went unto the bad
Had the good not held them in check.

I thought of all the swear words
That in my life I'd heard,
I hope I did not say them
I "do upon my word."
I rather think I did not,
But the tongue is an unruly member
I am somewhat like the "Bad Boy,"
I do not now remember.

Now when we had them "culprits" jailed
Put up their prison bars
The bell had rung for dinner twice
I feared domestic jars;
For if there's anything in this world
That makes my good wife scold
It's waiting dinner for a time
Till everything is cold. --

Now who is that a turning in,
A trotting up the drive?
It is Parson L., I'll bet my boots,
It is as I am alive.
The miserable V— why did he come?
When the weather is so fine,
His business could as well be done
In not so hurrying a time.

"Very glad to see you Parson L.,
Although I may be a sinner,
Just put your horse right in the barn
And stop with us to dinner."
"It can't be noon," the Parson said,
And his eyes they flashed amaze,
Then from his pocket drew his watch,
Then to the sun did gaze.

"Then from his pocket drew his watch,
Then to the sun did gaze."

Oh! Time flies fast in these lightning times.
In these fast living days,"
And the smiles danced on his pleasant face
Like the white caps on the waves.
"Yes I'll take you at your word
And to "dinner" with you stay,
Just throw the horse a peck of oats
You need not mind the hay."

My Wife came out upon the stoop,
She said not a word I think,
But quicker than a flash of light
She caught my little "wink."

I kept the Parson from the house
I showed him the calves and pig,
While my Wife she shuffled into
A cleaner and better rig.

I showed him the fine points of my nags
Told the feats that they'd perform,
And the number of years that had fled by
Since them two nags were born.
While in the house the dishes flew
Old table-cloth and all,
These being replaced by better ones
In honor of this call.

I told him that near nag of mine
In a race had been a winner,
And was interrupted in my tale
By a call of Wife to dinner.
When all were seated round the "board"
I gave the Parson a nod,
And he proceeded in a solemn tone
Returning thanks to God.

When our repast was ended
I felt I could not wait,
I thought I'd take my usual smoke,
Asked the Parson to "partake."
"No, thank you friend, I do not smoke
Narcotics I do not need,
No, for their use, I've no excuse,
It would be sowing "bad seed."

Now, while you enjoy this pleasure,
Draw solace from the "weed,"
I'll discourse to you a spell
About things I think we need.
It may not be a personal sin
For you to enjoy your smoke,
But there are weaker brethren in the line
That cannot stand the stroke.

And when once their appetites are 'roused
There is created a burning thirst,
That will not quench until they pass
From bad unto the worst.
Through all my life I have observed
Among all its whirl or din
That what's an innocent pleasure to one
To another may be a sin.

I think 'twould be by far the best
To fulfill the law to the "letter,"
And that we should let this pleasure go
For others it would be better.
Now Farmer D. you have prospered
By the tilling of the sward,
Now he that 'giveth to the poor
But lendeth to the Lord.'

There are many people in the world
To whom the "Word" was never preached
There are many people on this earth
The Bible has not reached.

The Word of God it teaches
And the mandate it is strong,
That the good has got to conquer
And must supplant the wrong.

This world of ours is beautiful
Which the Lord our God has given,
And promised if we are dutiful
We shall live with him in Heaven.
And one of our duties here to do
Is to help His noble Cause,
And snatch as many as we can
From sins most ragged jaws.

The people here upon this plain
Their old Church now do rue,
And think of erecting in its place
One that's good and new.
We cannot build this church with faith,
We cannot make it of prayer,
But we must have the solid *cash*;–
Now have you some to spare?—

For just as true, as the sky is blue,
And drops do form the river,
Blessings pure, that will endure
Shall be the reward of the giver.
Though you don't train under our Sectional Flag
Your aims are for the right,
And I have no doubt, but you are on your route
To Heaven's Mansions bright.

I think it would be by far the best
If you would join *our* Army Corpse
And march with us to the home of the just
Far away on the other shore.
Now Farmer D. upon these points
I wish you would speak your mind,
And tell me true, how it is with you
And how you are inclined."

I laid my pipe upon the shelf
And then I scratched my head,
And as my thoughts came to me
I finally spoke and said:
"I believe in the Gospel Banner
Though I don't live up to the text,
And that the God who made this world
Did also make the next.

That we all have duties here to do
That we should try and well perform
And make it our aim to Heaven gain
And escape the place that's "*warm*."
And to carry on this Gospel Work
It takes the cash I am well aware,
And as our Father deals with us
With Him we ought to share.

That the man that preaches the Word
Says mass and makes a prayer,
Has got a stomach like myself
And cannot live on air.

And like me he is also human
And with the flesh he has to fight,
And that he makes his "little mistakes"
While trying to serve the right.

I hardly think there is any Sect
That controls this "*Great Through Line*."
Or has any special bargain made
For making "quicker time."
I hardly think there is any Sect
That owns a Palace Car.
That will carry its members to Heaven's gates
Without a single jar.

I hardly think there is any Train
That runs upon the Rail.
But if it travels by the *Chart*
That Heaven's Hosts will hail.
I hardly think there is any Train
When all its passengers are in,
But has on board with all its good
Some of Adam's sin.

I don't believe their is any Train
That on this Track should run,
That carries only the great in mind
And slights the little one.
I don't believe upon this Track
And it seems its clear enough,
That the "Engine" makes the quickest time
That has the loudest puff.

I don't believe upon this Track
And it is very plain I ween,
That the "Engine is the strongest
That has the loudest scream.

I believe that every "Sleeper" on this route, No matter to what Train hitched, Before it arrives at the end of the Line, Will from the Track be switched.

I believe that every "*Sleeper*" on this Route

No matter to what Train hitched,
Before it arrives at the end of the Line
Will from the Track be switched.

I believe that the Lord who surveyed this Route
And superintends this Line,
Will see that every Train that runs
Shall make its proper time.
Nor is there any passenger
Who has a pass clear through,
But if he disobeys the rules
It will be cancelled ere he is due.

That the passenger who pays his fare,
Has his tickets "properly punched,"
Will find at the Lord's table a chair,
And "milk and honey" for lunch.
That paying the fare is "doing right,"
That the "checks" are the witnesses within,
That he has passed from "death to life"
Been freed from original sin.

"I believe this track which Moses laid,
And which our Savior did repair.

I believe this track which Moses laid,
And which our Savior did repair,
Is the only way that we are sure
Will ever lead us "There."
If there's an engine on this line,
And there are some, I ween,
That has not capacity enough
For making sufficient steam:—

It had better be voted from the Track
As a "sluggard" and a "harmer,"
And would better serve the human race
As a ditcher or a farmer.

It had better be voted from the track
As a "sluggard" and a "harmer,"
And would better serve the human race
As a ditcher or a farmer.

Now, Parson L., take no offense
At what to you I've said,
We all have got our duties to do,
We all have got to be fed.

Some are called to preach the Word,
Some in the busy marts to stand,
And some to settle up the feuds,
While others till the land.
Some there are who have nothing to do,
And I am sometimes led to think
That their only special calling is
To gape, and stretch, and blink.

Now, Parson L., when you've been the rounds
Of your own particular sect,
And in the end you lack a bit,
Why, then I'll draw my "check."
I am willing to do what ere is right
To help this noble cause,
For I believe it's the corner stone
Of all good and noble laws.

"Now, Farmer D., I agree with thee
In many things you say,
But there are some, I vow! I vum!
I see in a different way.
I wont stop now to argue these,
For I must wend my way,
But, perhaps, dear sir, the time may occur
When I'll have more to say.

Accept my thanks my Honored Host
And about that matter you spoke,
From what I've heard, I'd as soon have your word
As your "Promise to pay" in a note.
May the blessings of Heaven shine on you,
May your labors be met with reward,
May you enjoy this life in full measure
And in the end find a home with the Lord."

Dan had the Parsons rig to the door,
For a moment he did loiter,
Then stammering unto Dan he said:
"Did you give the horse some water?"
Dan in the affirmative did reply.
A smile played round the Parson's face.
He buttoned his duster good and high
And into his gig he jumped with grace.

He pulled the lap robe up in front
In the left hand held the rein,
Then turned his eye, gazed at the sky
And remarked, "It looks like rain."
Then with his whip, gave the horse a clip
Then uttered a solemn, "Steady! Whoa!"
Then waved his hand, and touched his hat
And bowed a kind "Good Day."

It was half past two, when the Parson went
And waved his farewell adieu;
But I *do* think, that Parsons *should think*
When "Haying Time" is due,

And take to themselves a vacation
Retire to Nature's charming bower,
Drink in her inspiration true.
To use in some dark hour.

"Now Dan if you ever made a motion
Since you have lived with me,
Hitch up them horses lively
And about that hay we'll see."
There comes my favorite Peddler
All prepared a trade "to whack,"
With fifty pounds in either hand
And twice that number on his back.

He thinks that labor is a sin
That a farmer is a plodder
And with his pack strapped on his back
He tries to get his fodder.
He would not plough, hoe nor mow,
He thinks it allied with trouble,
But makes a freight car of himself
Till he is bent up double.

And when adding up within his mind
His many little gains,
He gives no credit to muscle and bone,
But ascribes it all to brains.
How are you? Mr. Peter Pulkahetzel!
But I had almost rather be bounced,
In fact, be hung, than with the English tongue
To try and your name pronounce.

38

"Oh! the world moves fairly on vid me.
I have no cause for complain;
I makes my leetle trades each day,
And makes my leetle gains.
Do you vant any goods to-day?
I'll sell them very scheep,
For I have a "Pill" that's valling due,
And vhich I vants to meet.

"I bo't these goods of a Bankrupt Firm
For a leetle of nothing, sure,
They are goot to vear; they will not tear.
I'll warrant 'em to endure."
"Oh! Trade with the woman if you can.
For I've no time to linger,
And then I whispered unto wife
"Don't buy anything, by ginger!"

Here comes the Butcher looking for beef.
The red faced jolly clown,
He is coming now to buy that cow
I spoke about when at town.
"Well how is it with thee, Mr. Farmer D.,
And how about that cow?
As I was going by, I thought I'd try
If I could buy her now."

"Oh! Drive on your nag, and call again,
I have no time to dicker,
I would not stop now to sell a cow
Not even if it was my "kicker."

And then I whispered unto wife, " Don't buy anything, by ginger!"

"Beef's on the downward slide my friend
I suppose you well do know,
It's not worth now into a cent a pound
What it was a week. ago."

Here comes a man a selling tin
To barter for copper and rags,
And by the way we look, we'll be mistook,
He will have us all in bags.
Just then the maid came to the door
In a dress of old "Dolly Varden."
Cries she, "Your pigs are dancing jigs,
All over the best of your garden."

"Come Peddler of tin and notions too,
Come Butcher and let us try,—
Oh I hate a hog! Come here my dog,
Let us get them pigs in the sty."
In the English tongue, there are no words
To express the noise them pigs did make;
But peal on peal of terrific squeals
Did through the air vibrate.

On the waves of the wind, the fearful din
Did float away into space,
While the yelling of men and the bark of dog
Did follow quick in pace.
On each wave of the breeze, went a whee and a
    wheeze!
With a groan, a grunt and an Ug!
While each pig faced about presenting his snout
To be hit on the end with a club.

I know that the Creator of All Good
In his works never used any "Shoddy,"
But for all I have said, it seems a hog's head

"On each wave of the breeze, went a whee and a wheeze!
With a groan and a grunt and an Ug!
While each pig faced about, presenting his snout
To be hit on the end with a club!

Is on the wrong end of its body.
For backward they went, what ere their intent
Till they backed clear into the pen,
And when they were there, by their acts did
    declare
How came we here? and when?

I hardly could see in my life before
How the Devils entered the swine,
But now I'm content, they certainly went
In obediance to that summons *Divine*.
And though we are informed in *Scriptural Lore*
That them swine ran into the sea,
And of the devilish pack ne'er one came back
Oh how can all this this be?

For whatever with swine you have to do
Be your actions good or evil,
They will pay you back in every act
As if possessed of the D   — —.
Now I understand that saying of old.
"As contrary as a hog on ice,"
And can plainly see, it will lasting be
As, So Bossy! So- o! Hoist!

"I thank you friends each and all
For the service you have given,
Thus in helping another, out of a bother
You have fulfilled the Law of Heaven.   .
As you each ply well your special trade
May plenty crown your store,
You have my good will, that your money till.
May be full and running oe'r.

Ah!   Here comes a stranger through the gate
With portly look,   aye grand,
With massive brow and comely shape
And gloves upon his hand.

"Good Day, my friend! Do I now address
Mr. Farmer D. his honored self?"
"You have that honor, if it an honor be
Though with the honored I'm only an elf."

"I would like to speak with you my friend
In private if you please,
And when planned aright and you join in might
We will launch it on the breeze."
"We will hie to the barn my honored friend
The Farmer's "Office" you understand,
Now make yourself at home, at ease.
I am your "servant" and at your command."

"My friends they say, and seem sincere,
That they think it for the public good,
That I should feast for at least a year
Upon the government's food.
It is a fact, as you well know,
That them old laws our fathers made
Are getting almost obsolete,--
They are very old and staid.

They need remodling, "fixing up"
They are too slow a "team,"
They do not with the times keep pace
Of Telephone and Steam.
I feel ordained by Providence
That this is my "special work"
I have felt its impress ere so long
That from the "field" I dare not shirk.

I intend to enter the canvass
"*Solely* for the public good.
(Aside.) But within I have a "hankering"
By us "Statesmen" understood)
I will stand by my "Constituents"
(Aside.) But the "Lobby" I admire)
I will stand by my "Constituents"
(Unless there is something *hire—er.*

I want your help now Farmer D.,
Though you and I are strangers
And you may bet I'll try and skin my eye
For the good of all the "Grangers."
Now will you give me your word of honor
Your honor as a man,
That you will help me in this matter
And do whatso'ere you can.

"Now Hon. A. I will say to you
Our Country does stand in need
Of remedies that are healing
It is late in the day to "bleed."
But in all our Nation's "ailments"
For all of her seeming "ills",
I think the "*Doctors*" do her "bleed,"
As often as they give "healing pills,"

Now in the early days of our Nation's life
The office sought the man,
And there were but few, that made up the crew
Now styled the "Political Band,"

"We will hie to the barn, my honored friend, The Farmers 'office' you understand. Now make yourself at home, at ease, I am your 'servant' and at your command."

But in these days when a noble soul
Sees his country going to ruin,
And knows from that hour, if placed in power
He can stay the storm that's brewing,

He must have money at his command
And influence "high" I remark.
And some to yell "Sic Him!" "Sterboy!"
And some to run and bark.
He has got to "own" a pack of hounds
Strong in muscle, might and main
Commanded by a "huntsman true"
That knows where to find the "game."

One that knows well the "hunting ground,"
And the favorite haunts of "game,"
If he would have luck, to follow his pluck,
And wishes to "hole" the same.
Now, brains enough I have not got
To help you pull the wire,
My budget of influence it is small,
It will not pay to hire.

My pace is slow, at any rate,
It is only a farmer's jog,
And I cannot see what I can be
Unless I can be your—dog.
I have barked around the "political stump!"
When told that there was "game,"
But I'll be bound, some other 'hound'
Did always get the same.

"I have barked around the "political stump."

I have fought for these political "bricks".
With the spirit of a Spartan -aye, bolder,
And was led to think, by *promise* and *wink*,
That they would bear the *Nation on their shoulder*
Bear her up through the quags and mires,
Stop the wasting of her sweetest sip,
And land her at last, as in a mother's grasp,
In the *Goddess of Liberty's l p*.

I watched my "model" of political skill,
Take the Nation on his shoulder,
And was proud at heart to see him start,
For the "Goddess," to enfold her,
My pulse beat slow, my heart throbbed low,
As his form became unsteady,
I saw him reel, slip on Bribery's "peel",
Go down in corruption's eddy.

No, to you I will make no promises,
On my help you need not dote;
But it belongs to me, to carefully see
Where goes my honest vote.

"Take the Nation on his shoulder."

Now, Dan, that hay we now must get,
No matter what comes next;
We must not stop, unless we are bought,
For any slight pretext.

The *lungs* of *Nature*, which had heaved
The whole of the live-long day,

43

"My pulse beat slow, my heart throbbed low, As his form became unsteady."

And which had raised particular fits
When we were at the hay,
Had quieted down to their "normal state"
And ceased to moan and fret,
And the "symptoms" they were very strong,
That Nature was about to "sweat."

For in the South a bank of clouds
As black as nether doom,
With lightning flash, and then a crash
Of thunder's fearful boom,
Proclaimed to me, as plain could be
Without a revelation,
That the clouds were about to empty out
On earth their "perspiration."

We had that jag re-loaded,
And we were ready to go;
The sky was black as dooms-Day
Three Dooms-days in a row.
The drops came down with terrific force
From Heaven's Hydraulic Ram,
And it seemed by the roaring, hissing sound
They had broke away the "dam."

Each drop was a *little winter*,
As it struck our *summer wear*,
It made a *snow-drift* of our feelings,
An *iceberg* of each hair.
Into the barn we drove pell mell,
A yelling like two country bricks,
Ran through an old hen and chickens
And killed just three of them chicks.

Down came the rain in torrents
In drops both large and small,
It wet the hay and everything
The eaves were a waterfall;

I sought my cot in the kitchen
With feelings any but grand,
And to ease my pain took the very first train
To dreamland's happy land.

And in that beautiful world of visions
To my hearts content and delight
I found they had not a "*Day*" that's "*Bad*"
But one most lovingly bright.
I thought it was in "Haying Time"
Quite early in the morn
And as I cast my eye unto the sky
There were no signs of "storms."

And though the "Almanac" it had said
"The sun will rise at half past Four."
It seemed to me, it was up at Three
And had opened wide its door,
Thrown back the "shutters" of the night
Rolled up the "curtains" high
And with its radiant beams did light
The whole of the Eastern sky.

I thought the "cows" came up alone
Came one by one to me,
And stood so still, while my pail did fill
I'd only to look on and see.
I thought "Old Brin" was the first to come
I thought she was not lame,
All seemed right, and the sky was bright
And it did not look like rain.

I thought my dog lay close to me
All curled up in a little heap,
And in dog language seemed to say
"I have not chased any sheep."

I thought neighbor Fry, he was at home
And with convulsions did quiver,
I thought the nurse was dosing him
With medicine for his *liver*.

I thought my "nags" came trotting up
All hitched to a new hay rig,
With Dan, my man, to them command
While he was dancing a jig.
I thought the cows they grazed around
And chewed their cuds in the shade,
Remaind in view, did not fret or stew
As if they thought to aid.

It seemed the "Peddlers" went straight by,
They never look our way,
As if they thought that we had got
To handle all that hay.

I rocked my "Pet Child" some that day,
Snatched kisses of approbation,

I thought the "Parson" he went by
On his way to spend "Vacation."

But from these thoughts I suddenly woke,
Pleasant dream it was to me ,
As my little Daughter to me spoke
And says "Pa' get up to tea."
And having done justice to that meal
Regaled the inner man.
We all went out to milk the cows
And Dan did lead the van.

But ere I fairly had commenced,
Oh how their tails did fly,
And straightway with unerring aim
They took me in the eye.
And though the sun was shining bright
All through the window bars,
I could distinctly, plainly see
The "Twinkling of the stars."

And if they chanced to miss my "eye"
Though they would scarcely ever fail,
Then backward in its course 'twould come
Co—slap into the pail.
All reeking with this milky foam
Then came what I did fear,
And with a true unerring aim
She "swashed" it in my ear.

I thought of that fanatic fool
Who by his close devotion
Had ruined his reason and body too
In seeking "Perpetual Motion,"
And wished he were there for a little spell
I know he would have recovered,
For he'd have thought, he'd certainly got
What ne'r had been discovered.

Oh how I wish "my kicker" was milked!
I wish to the "Butcher" I'd sold her,
And you may bet I will, or call me a pill
Before I am very much older.
But sighing and wishing amounts to naught
In this world's busy strife,
So down to "my kicker" I immediately got
After saying "Good Bye" to Wife.

"What are you about?" I yelled quite loud
With thoughts nigh unto sinning
"What ails your pegs, keep still your legs,
Keep down your underpinning."
She stood in a twice, as still as mice.
And gently chewed her cud,
From me not a word, there was nothing stirred
Except the milk's dull thud.

When quicker than a flash, there came a crash,
Like the banging of a door,
The milk did fly and so did I,
All sprawled upon the floor.

I gathered my bones up in a heap
Placed them down on stable sill,
And could you have seen my face just then
You'd thought I was making my " *Will*."

And if that subject had been my theme
I give to you my vow,
That the man I hated the worst on earth
I'd willed to him that cow.
And the principal tenet of that "will"
And the sole condition on which made,
That he should milk her *twice* a day
While on this earth she stayed.

The worst punished man in all this world
This enemy of mine would have been,
He'd wished Satan had come from his abode
And took him to live with him.
States-prison would been a place of joy
With rounds of pleasure I'll allow,
And hanging a "sweet sensation"
In place of milking that cow.

"Dan," I cried in anguish tones,
"My Stalwart Dan I trow,
If you have any conceit you can't be beat,
Just try and finish that cow.
My bones are sore and so is my grit
My nerves are all unstrung,
And curses not few, my mind course through,
Though I've uttered ne'r a one."

"Now Boss I vow, and do declare
By all that's said and writ,
That whatever I thought that you might lack
I never supposed it was grit.
There never was a cow in this broad land
Composed of muscle, bones and meat,
That when once I was seated by her side
Did ever me unseat.

I will finish that cow for you my Bess
I will, as I'm a man.
And when she is done, as Number One
You shall sip the health of Dan."
With muscle of steel, and a heart of flint
That in fierce fight would never fail,
Dan seated himself beside that cow,
And the milk went bubbling in the pail.

Quiet reigned supreme, like the gentle lull
That follows in the wake of the dread storm's
        blast;
A deathly stillness reigned o'er all
As Dan continued at his task.
The milk had almost ceased to flow,
The finishing stroke was near,
When quicker by far, than a "shooting star"
Dan landed on his ear.

"*Great Guns!*" he cried, "Is it the End of Time?
Has the Judgement certainly come?
What is that roaring in my ear?

"The milk had almost ceased to flow. The finishing stroke was near.
When quicker by far, than a "shooting star" Dan landed on his ear."

Is it the sound of Trumpet and Drum?"
Then into a limpsy mass he fell,
The color from his face did go,
And the expression on his countenance le t
Bespoke his fearful woe.

I bent o'er his still and stalwart form
I stroked his manly brow,
And as his consciousness did return
He gazed up to that cow.
"I swear by the Kings of Saturn
By the red faced firey Mars.
By all the Planets that in space revolve
By the Universe of stars.

By all the bovines of the land
That do earth's waters quaff,
That there is "*Lightning*" enough in that cow's
    hide
To run the whole "*Telegraph.*"
If I owned that cow myself Boss,
Whether low in this world's goods or up
I'd trade her off for something else
If it was naught but a "poodle pup."'

"Dan, let others prate the gentleness
Of our Yankee bovine race,
But you'll agree, I trust with me
That they'll depopulate our race.
People may talk about the Farmer,
Of his comforts and his joys,
Of his merry laughing milkmaids
And his jolly whistling boys,

Of the breezy air of freedom
That surround their country's home,
As through the vales they ramble,

Or o'er the hills they roam.
But among all this joy and gladness
There are some things that are sad
Among all these days of goodness
There is often one that's "*Bad.*"

It was in July and Haying Time
Just at the close of day,
I had fed the pigs and done the chores
And turned the cows away,
The sun sank low in the distant west
To sleep in Morpheus' arm,
And with its last departing ray
Closed the "*Bad Day On The Farm.*"

FINIS.

AGENTS

WANTED in every town and county in the United States to sell "BAD DAY ON THE FARM." Send twenty-five cents for "Prospectus" and outfit and go to work. You will find it the best seilling Book of the season. It needs only to be shown to sell it. Sample copies of "BAD DAY ON THE FARM," sent to any address post paid on receipt of retail price (50 cts.) fifty cents. Liberal terms to agents. Correspondence solicited. All communications should be addressed to the Author, (who owns and controls the whole business, having hired the printing of the same at so much (per thousand.)

M. F. BENTLEY,
Canton, St. Lawrence Co., N. Y.